TAKE THE LEAD

ALTO SAXOPHONE

Bumper Book

Editorial, production and recording: Artemis Music Limited (www.artemismusic.com) • Published 2005

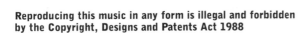

Angels

Demonstration: CD1
Backing: CD2

Words and Music by Robert Williams
and Guy Chambers

Rather slow

Blueberry Hill

Demonstration: CD1
Backing: CD2

Words and Music by Al Lewis,
Vincent Rose and Larry Stock

Careless Whisper

Demonstration: CD1
Backing: CD2

Words and Music by George Michael
and Andrew Ridgeley

Rather Slow

Come Away With Me

Demonstration: CD1
Backing: CD2

Words and Music by Norah Jones

Dance Of The Sugar Plum Fairy

Music by Pyotr Ilych Tchaikovsky

Demonstration: CD1
Backing: CD2

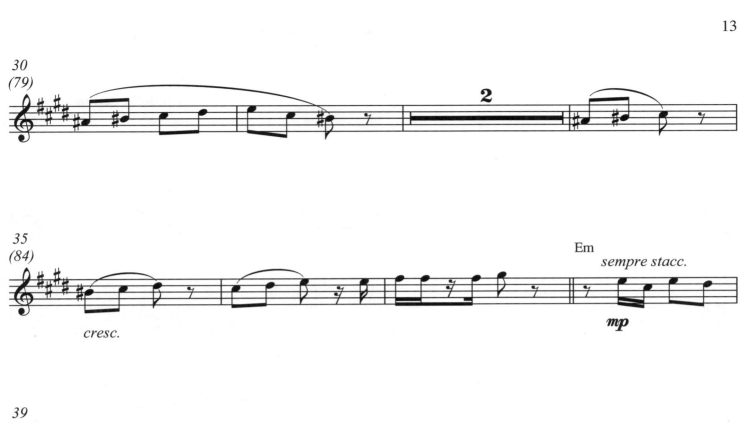

Everybody Needs Somebody To Love

Demonstration: CD1
Backing: CD2

Words and Music by Bert Burns,
Solomon Burke and Jerry Wexler

Fascinating Rhythm

Demonstration: CD1
Backing: CD2

Music and Lyrics by George Gershwin
and Ira Gershwin

Guantanamera

Demonstration: CD1
Backing: CD2

Words and Music by Diaz Fernandez

I'll Be There For You

Demonstration: CD1
Backing: CD2

Words and Music by
Phil Solem, Marta Kauffman, David Crane,
Michael Skloff, Allee Willis and Danny Wilde

Bright rock

La Bamba

Traditional
Arranged by Ritchie Valens

Demonstration: CD1
Backing: CD2

In The Mood

Demonstration: CD1
Backing: CD2

Words by Andy Razaf
Music by Joe Garland

28

My Heart Will Go On

Words by Will Jennings
Music by James Horner

Demonstration: CD1
Backing: CD2

Over The Rainbow

Demonstration: CD1
Backing: CD2

Words by E Y Harburg
Music by Harold Arlen

Ballad tempo

Singin' In The Rain

Words by Arthur Freed
Music by Nacio Herb Brown

Demonstration: CD1
Backing: CD2

Medium swing

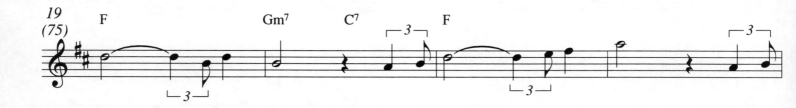

Sound Of The Underground

Demonstration: CD1
Backing: CD2

Words and Music by Brian Higgins,
Niara Scarlett and Miranda Cooper

Driving rock tempo

Star Wars (Main Theme)

Music by John Williams

Demonstration: CD1
Backing: CD2

Summer Nights

Demonstration: CD1
Backing: CD2

Words and Music by Jim Jacobs
and Warren Casey

Summertime
(From Porgy And Bess®)

Music and Lyrics by George Gershwin,
Du Bose Heyward, Dorothy Heyward
and Ira Gershwin

Demonstration: CD1
Backing: CD2

Uptown Girl

Words and Music by Billy Joel

Demonstration: CD1
Backing: CD2

Moderate rock & roll

When You Say Nothing At All

Demonstration: CD1
Backing: CD2

Words and Music by Paul Overstreet
and Don Schlitz

48